SICK

LIKE

ME

K.L. TAYLOR-LANE

ISBN - 978-1-917276-02-3
Written by - K.L. Taylor-Lane
Cover Design by - Dee Garcia, Black Widow Designs

Author's Note

This is a dark, forbidden, enemies-to-lovers, gothic, MF romance.

This is a short story.

This book is written in British English. Therefore, some spellings, words, grammar and punctuation may be used differently than what you are used to.

Please be aware this book contains dark themes and subjects that may be uncomfortable/unsuitable for some readers. This book contains heavy themes throughout so please heed the warning and go into this with your eyes wide open.

For more detailed information, please see full content listing.

The characters in this story all deal with trauma and problems differently, the resolutions and methods they use are not always traditional and therefore may not be for everyone.

Caelus

I

Blackgrave Academy is best at night. Rigid and imposing, the castle stands in the centre of misty moorlands, directly between two dense forests on either side, each one of them belonging to opposing, old money families.

The huge, stone structure is formidable. Every column and pillar wrapped in vines. Twin gargoyle statues guarding the gates from high above, their aged, grey eyes tracking every person that enters through the wrought-iron entrance.

Moonlight beams down onto the grounds as I start to make my way out of the rear entrance. Fog cools my overheated skin as it curls around my ankles, the damp air pricking goosebumps along my forearms, rippling up to my exposed biceps.

I'm not going to have a lot of time to deal with this. I've just finished teaching my ten-pm class, and now I'm trudging my way into the woods, wearing ballet tights, trainers and a fucking stringer vest, to deal with a problem for my father.

Branches slap at my bare arms as I manoeuvre my way through Carnell Wood. Sweat sticks the flimsy, thin cotton of my vest top to my back, the early summer wind cooling my hot, damp skin as I inhale the thick scent of fir trees carried on the breeze. Rustling leaves and snapping twigs are the only sounds I detect atop my hard breaths and the pound of my heart buzzing in my ears.

That's why it's such a surprise to find her here.

There are many cabins and crumbling old cottages out here in these woods, but something there absolutely should not be on my family's land, is a Stone.

Moonlight catches her familiar white-blonde hair as it breaks through the canopy of Oaks and Birch, turning it a silvery grey. Her skin is much the same, making her appear sallow and ghoul-like, carving her side profile up like a haunting skeleton mask.

I study her movements as she approaches the man, whispering words I am unable to hear from this distance. The man says nothing, but that's enough to capture my attention.

Wesley Clarke.

At twenty-five years old, he's a failed-professional footballer with a giant chip on his shoulder because he made his daddy bank when he took over a big chunk of west London by spilling copious amounts of what he calls 'designer heroin' onto the streets.

It doesn't impress me, but the way in which *she* moves does.

Elegantly pressing up onto her dainty toes, her feet arching into a slender curl, her calf muscles tensing, knees straightening, all of it prominent to me even beneath the thick material of her black leggings. Her thighs tighten, and even without using her hands, she is perfectly balanced, her core muscles keeping her still and upright. It takes some dancers years to perfect that, but without any practice at all, she holds it.

Her long, thin fingers come to the front of Wesley's shoulders, the tips just barely pressing against them, but he's enthralled by her in the same way as I. His eyes are on the stretched length of her slender body. She's five-ten to his six-one, so she's not far away from her target with those toxic lips. His eyes are already shuttering, lids only half open as she leans in, allowing his hands to land on her hips, but I catch the small tremor that runs through her as they do.

It makes my teeth grind.

Especially when her mouth finally brushes his.

Immediately, he tries to deepen the chaste kiss, his lips parting, fingers tightening on the flare of her hips, but she doesn't allow it, settling back on her heels. She blinks up at him in the way she always does, this innocent little flutter of lashes, a blank look, something I am all too intimately familiar with.

That's how they stay for too many minutes. Locked in an embrace, him holding her, her hands resting delicately against the front of his shoulders, his back to a tree. He speaks lowly, a murmuring, their lips too close, sharing breath, and she listens, keeping a small distance, enough not to touch, but never replies.

Finally, when my short nails cut into my palms, blood filling the underside of my nails where I fist my hands so tightly, she steps back, breaking his hold on her as he coughs. A dry sort of throat clearing, just the once.

"Ostara," he splutters quickly, shooting heat through my veins like strikes of lightning at hearing him call her name like that. "What the fuck did you do?" he asks immediately, his voice low, a disbelieving whisper.

Knowing, I'm sure, as well as everyone else on this campus, that Ostara Stone has a dark little secret, and he just found out exactly what it is.

Poison.

Only, he won't ever be able to share it with anyone now. So, her secret will stay just that, and he will die, realising in his final moments, just how stupid he was to underestimate her. In the same way that everyone else always does.

"You're sick, Ostara!" he shouts, shoving at her small frame with his much larger one. "Fucking sick!"

To her credit, she doesn't let it affect her, she doesn't fall or twist or stumble, she simply glides back, her white, high tops smoothing through the dewy foliage, so she's a few safe feet away.

"Bye bye, Wesley," she says then, this lyrical little whisper that she completes with a head tilt.

The idiot drops to his knees, his hand to his throat as he gasps for air. And Ostara, she stands there, just out of his reach, wiping the white cuff of her sweatshirt across her pretty, red-stained mouth. It smears across her cheek before she cleans it off completely. And then, still staring at the man, white foam starting to fizz from his mouth, blood seeping from his bulging eyes, a sharp, gurgling, hiss escaping his chest. She lifts the small vial attached to a long silver chain, concealed beneath the neckline of her oversized sweatshirt to her lips and swallows its contents.

Slowly, re-tucking the chain beneath her clothing once more, she turns her head towards me, her sapphire blue eyes darkening as the moon's beams disappear behind a cloud, leaving us in shadow, and Wesley's head thuds against the ground.

"Caelus," she greets politely, like we're old friends.

We're not, despite the way we keep meeting in the dark, pulled towards one another like lost spirits finding the light.

"You shouldn't be here," I rumble, my voice a deep, low warning, that doesn't have the desired effect.

"Why not?" she asks whimsically, her body still angled away from me, hands relaxed by her sides, head canted, that siren blue gaze on me from the corner of her eye.

"Because this is Carnell land, Miss Stone," I tell her more sharply.

Irritation flaring beneath the sudden tightness of my skin, that's how it always is around her, a hatred carved so deep into my bones that it's settled in my marrow. She smiles then, tipping her head further right, angling herself so she can look at me more fully, her chin brushing her shoulder.

"That could be argued, though," she replies softly, "couldn't it, *Master* Carnell?" she mocks with a tinkling laugh that hits me right in the balls.

Anger thrums just beneath the surface of my light skin, skin that suddenly feels like it's not quite my own whilst I'm in the presence of this girl. This twenty year old fucking nightmare with poison laced lips and a blank stare that makes the hair raise on the back of my neck and my heart pound inside my chest like a battering ram trying to crack through my ribcage.

It's why I stay away from her.

Ostara Stone makes me forget myself.

And that's just about the most dangerous thing that could ever happen to me.

When I stride towards her, closing the too large, yet too small, distance between us, I'm honing in on her like a predator. Every instinct screaming at me to kill. My natural born enemy, my grandfather's once-best friend's granddaughter, the rival blood to everything I know. She is as forbidden to me as I am to her.

Which is why we always meet this way.

Nothing ever happens.

But she speaks to me.

And she never communicates with anyone, not anyone she plans to keep alive anyway.

Except for me.

Suddenly, we are a collision.

The way our teeth clash as we come together, her hands claw at my bare shoulders, nails cutting in deep, as my fingers dig into the soft flesh of her arse. She's light in my arms, tasting sweet and impermissible, and I lap at her mouth like it's melting ice cream as I heft her up high into my arms.

The wrap of her long legs twining around my waist, the rubber soles of her shoes jabbing into the tops of my glutes, dragging me into her as we fall against a tree. My cock is hard, weeping at the tip, and her hips are rolling, grinding and crushing her cunt against the ladder of my abs, bunching the very light fabric of my stringer vest up between us.

She hisses as I bite her bottom lip, tasting the bitter remnants of her poison-tinged weapon. It isn't something I stop to think about though, the fear of death. Not with the heat of her pussy rubbing against me, her nails drawing blood down the juts of my shoulder blades. The scent of her arousal seeps through the stretchy material of her leggings, my nostrils flaring in the cold wind as I bite off our kiss. Dipping my face down into the hollow of her throat and curling my tongue up the length of her bared neck.

Her head drops back as I suck on the underside of her chin, swirling my tongue around the clamped circle of the inside of my teeth. She grunts as I bite into her, the hollow space not much more than skin and bone, so I know it hurts. It doesn't stop her though, a whimper dropping from her throat, quickly stripped away by the whip of the summer breeze. Her knees tighten against the ridges of my rib bones, heels digging in harder against my lower spine.

"Cal," she breathes, her eyes opening as I release my bite on her chin, licking up the length of her jaw.

Those long, skilled fingers claw upwards of the muscles in the top of my back, dragging sharply into my thick mess of dark brown hair, the curves of her nails breaking the skin of my scalp.

"Ozzie," I bite into her neck, my hazel eyes flicked up on her blues. "Tell me to stop."

I demand it like I would do it.

Stop.

Even though I wouldn't.

We are destruction.

The third eldest daughter to the Stones.

The third eldest son to the Carnells.

Neither one of us particularly important.

Enemies and so much more than that.

There are lies and betrayal and backstabbing that runs far deeper than either her or I could even dream.

But this, the wetness seeping through her leggings, sinking into the flimsy cotton of my baggy top, her tongue twisting around mine as our mouths inevitably connect once again, this is not something that's supposed to happen.

Her teeth nip the tip of my tongue sending a jolt of need straight down into the pit of my stomach. Heat flares across my eyelids as I clench my eyes shut.

"No," she finally whispers against my

tongue, the tinge of copper in the back of my throat. I'm a runaway train off of its track heading straight for the edge of a cliff, "No, Cal," she whines lowly. "Don't stop."

And I don't.

One of my hands snakes up her spine beneath the heavy fabric of her sweatshirt, stepping back from the tree. My fingers twist in the band of her bra, drawing it away from the bumps of her spine just enough to let it snap back against her as I let it go, forcing her to flinch closer, pressing her breasts up into my face.

"Get this off," I grunt, biting at the heavy material before she releases her claws from my scalp and lifts the bundle of white fabric over her head.

I bury my face in the crevice between her tits, lapping the flat of my tongue up the centre of her chest. Swirling the tip over the length of long silver chain hanging around her neck, and then slam her back against the tree.

Air huffs out of her nose at the impact, our mouths coming together once more before one of her hands is back, fisting in my hair and yanking violently on the sweaty, dark strands, tearing my head back.

Adam's apple bobbing in my throat with a dry swallow, my lips parted, I stare up into her eyes, sapphire blue carved with shadow, her cheekbones high and cupid's bow stained red.

"You're going to die tonight, Caelus," she whispers, thumbing across my plump bottom lip, before sucking the tip into her own mouth with an open eyed stare.

She's the definition of strange. Unusual in the way she speaks, her stares, the silence, her lonesome persona. She drifts like a spirit, floating through the academy halls, keeping to herself, attending no more than two classes a week, but she still has one of the most fearsome reputations Blackgrave Academy has ever seen.

It's part of the attraction I feel. Pulled into her orbit, only to be spun around and knocked eight feet to the left of her. Leaving me with dizziness and a brain fog with the ever present question of how the fuck does she draw me in?

We're enemies.

I hate her.

She hates me.

And yet, as her bare back scrapes up the rough bark of the tree, my mouth suctioning over her collarbone, teeth driving into the bone, marking her with the intent to scar, I forget all of that.

I forget the why.

I forget who I am.

Ozzie's legs tight around my waist, her back to the tree, pinned there by my weight, allows me to release my grip on her arse to fist the elastic material at her crotch and rip.

'You're going to die tonight, Caelus.'

"But not before I fuck you, you filthy little nightmare."

Ostara

II

Caelus' fingers suddenly drive into the sloppy state of my cunt like he's trying to fight his way inside of me, fist my soul and tear it out between my legs. My leggings are torn, gaping at the centre seams, allowing the cool air to rush across my oversensitive flesh.

The flinch can't be controlled, nor can the blush that flits to my cheeks, or the wanton cry that chokes its way up my throat like the jagged claws of a demon trying to escape my oesophagus. Stars shoot across my vision beneath the tight clench of my eyelids as my head thuds back against the large tree trunk.

"That's it, you murderous little ghoul, strangle my fingers," Cal huffs with an undertone of mockery, like we're playing a game he thinks he's just won.

But, despite the pleasure heating my lower belly, the cramp in my core muscles tightening and ricocheting all the way down to my bones, I'm having a mild panic. I think of the poison residue on my mouth, now on his, the empty vial of antidote squashed between my breasts.

I imagine the praise I'd receive, the third son to the Carnells, dead at my hands. They all think I'm disposable. The Stones. My *family.* Because of the way my brain is wired. It's why I was locked away for so long before being allowed out of the prison they call a home. They couldn't *trust* me to carry out my duties and behave like a normal person.

I had to earn my *freedom*.

I'm *still* earning my freedom.

Cal's a teacher at the academy, the ballet master, fourteen years my senior, and everything I'm supposed to hate, so what does it matter if I kill him?

It'd work in my favour, earn me some points with my father.

Perhaps.

But now, right now, I think I might be about to lose my virginity to one of the people they hate the most, that *I* should hate the most, and even as I think of killing him, I don't think I really could.

Caelus Carnell is the only person I have ever met that has never intentionally tried to hurt me. He's the only person I ever give the time of day to. Speak to. Our passing pleasantries, these lingering private moments where it's just the two of us in the dark, the quiet, are sometimes the only human interaction I get for weeks at a time. My teachers and peers, when I bother to attend any of my classes, don't even seem to see me. I am nothing more than a ghost flitting through the halls.

A shiver runs up my spine as Caelus brings his drenched digits up into the scant space between us, his hand dangerously close to his mouth and mine. I can smell the slick of my arousal mixing with his skin, his dark, masculine scent intoxicating with the combined sharpness of me. Laying those dangerous, freckled, hazel eyes on mine, he sucks his fingers between his lips and wraps his tongue around them. His cheeks hollow, his pale pink lips tight, suctioned up to the knuckle, he devours my flavour off of his skin, groaning as he does.

I should stop this now, launching myself off of a jagged cliff's edge, but when Cal's mouth comes back to mine, twining his tongue over my own, I forget myself.

How to think.

How to breathe.

Instead, all I can do is feel as the head of his weeping cock presses against my wet cunt, one of his hand's back on my fabric covered arse. The other curled beneath my left thigh, fingers splayed, thumb digging into the soft skin of my inner thigh, holding me open, my legs still wrapped around his waist.

"Ozzie," he breathes the name over my mouth, he's the only person to call me that, as though it's just between us, like we're more than meagre familiars. His lips pluck mine like delicate fingertips over harp strings, "Tell me you want this."

He holds my gaze with the demand, his

stare boring into me, waiting as his cock weeps fluid that sticks to the wet flesh of my pussy. I can hardly breathe as he looks at me, the tips of our noses brushing.

"I hate you," I whisper instead, something I'm supposed to feel, perhaps saying it aloud, making sure he hears, it'll make it real.

It'll make this moment real.

Because, sometimes, these moments are not.

I'm not always here, even when I am, and to find my way back I have to bleed.

"I hate you too," he breathes and then slams his cock inside of me.

Caelus pauses for just a second as he feels it, and then he forces himself through that tiny piece of resistance set high inside of me and fucks me like a wild beast.

He's savage and raw and I clench around him like I'm trying to draw him in deeper and simultaneously force him out. He grunts as my forehead drops to his in a crash, our skulls knocking together, my hands clawing at his shoulder blades, the curves of bone sawing into the soft palms of my hands.

Caelus pounds into me ruthlessly, his pelvis

grinding into my clit shooting little sparks of pleasure directly into the front of my skull. His hands simultaneously hold me up whilst tearing me apart, he fucks me just like he said. With hate. And I realise this is what I need.

This feeling.

Caelus' hate for me is so intense it's the first real thing I think I've ever felt.

It's heady, this sudden burst of intense emotion.

"Harder," I demand in a breathless whisper as my bottom lip trembles, a groan filling my throat that I try to fight, the taste as forbidden on my tongue as Caelus' flavour. "Make me hurt," *so I can feel.* "I hate you," I tell him again, my voice wobbly, trying to block out everything but this.

"I'm going to make you fucking bleed," he hisses into my ear before his teeth snap down on my earlobe and sink into the flesh.

His breath is hot down my neck, but the eruption of lava heat licking my core where his thick cock strokes a fire inside of me has me unable to focus on his face. Even as my eyes are wide open on his, my head spinning with ecstasy, I manage to wriggle a hand up between our connected bodies, my other clawing into the muscles of his back, and slap him across the face so hard it makes even my teeth rattle as his head snaps to the side.

Still, his thrusts never falter, his pale cheek burning bright, the shape of my hand quickly reddening his face. Slowly, his head turns back to me, his eyes on mine even before he's fully facing me again.

"You're finally playing the game, Ostara?" he asks with a slow stretching smirk, his voice like a bitter slap to my own face.

He circles his hips, grinding into me before he draws himself almost all the way and drops his gaze between us.

The sharp suction of air he inhales startles me, making me clench up around his tip even tighter, making him grunt, but he's not looking up at me as he stills completely. That has me dropping my gaze too, his silence.

Moonlight breaks through the canopy of branches overhead just enough that we're both able to see the veiny length of his thick cock streaked with red. He's so still for a moment, it reminds me of looking in a mirror, when I'm trying to come back to myself, grasp hold of reality, murder my vacant stare. And I wonder how to bring him back.

To this moment.

To me.

It feels frighteningly important that he's as present in this as I am.

This indiscretion that can only end one way.

Death.

Blood is the only thing that brings me back when I forget myself, but I have no blade, no dagger, no knife.

Reaching down between us, my other hand curling in the roots of his dark chocolate coloured hair, I swipe two fingers down the long length of his cock, tip still nestled inside of me, gathering the evidence of our hedo-nistic joining, and smear the bloody digits over his mouth.

Sharply, he sucks in air again, his gaze snapping up to meet mine as I push my fingers between his teeth, sliding them to the very back of his tongue, until his throat clenches around the tips of them with a gag. Cal's fingers clamp down on my wrist, and I think he's going to shove me away, drop me and run for the hills. Instead, he holds me to him, sucking on the taste of us, of my virginity, my need. His teeth bite down on my knuckles at the same time he plunges his way back inside me.

Spikes of pleasure crash through me and I cry out, my head thudding back once more as Cal picks up the pace, spits out my fingers, and thumbs my clit. My grip tightens in his hair, nails clawing into his scalp, my other hand curling around the side of his neck, my thumb pressing too hard against his Adam's apple.

"You took my kill," Caelus grits out, his voice hoarse where I apply more pressure to his throat. "Now you're paying for it," he grunts, my back scraping and snagging on the rough bark of the tree. "How's that feel, Oz? Knowing you gave up your virginity to your enemy in exchange for an easy kill?"

He stares at me, his cock like a steel rod of fire pounding into me. Hazel eyes freckled with deep, dark green smirk up at me as he pinches my clit, and I detonate around his still thrusting cock. A cry rips up my throat, my grip on his hair tearing him closer until his lips are wrapped around my pulse point and he's groaning against my skin, the vibration rocking through my skeleton and rotting in my marrow.

My cunt clenches around him, little spasms of pleasure rippling up from the base of my spine and settling in the crown of my head, forcing stars to shoot across my eyes, distorting my view of his perfect face with spots of black.

He's panting when his bite leaves my throat, red staining his perfect teeth as he smiles up at me.

"How was that, Ostara?"

His mouth tips up on one side, his head beginning to cant, so I release my hold on his hair, let my legs drop down from his back, and lift myself up and off of his cock.

When he releases his hold on me, letting my feet slowly sink to the ground, I reply, "Fine," and scoop down to grab my sweat-shirt, tugging it over my head.

Caelus doesn't move, doesn't speak, and I keep my eyes down as I flick my blonde hair out of the collar.

"*Fine?*" he snarls at my back as I turn away

from him, my head lifting just enough that I can flick my eyes to the top of their lids and see the moon breaking through the trees once more.

"You need to come with me for the antidote," I tell him quietly over my shoulder without looking back, even if it's only residual, it could be enough to kill him slowly. "Unless you really do want to die."

He is silent as I begin to walk away, his warm cum seeping out of me and wetting the inside of my thighs, my leggings torn, underwear shredded. Heart clattering like an unco-ordinated brass band inside my chest, I fight off the cold feeling cloaking me once again. Caelus' warmth disappears, slipping off of my skin like water as I continue stepping further away. It makes something inside of me hurt, more than the ache between my thighs, the muscle cramp in my belly. I ignore it all, even as it makes me wonder, as I wander through the firs and the pines, about death, if, like me, that's exactly what he wants.

Caelus

III

It's not usually something I think about. Someone touching a girl that doesn't belong to me.

Let alone one that hasn't stepped foot near me for weeks, no matter how often I track her down.

I've never given a fuck before. I've shared women with my brothers, both younger and older. I fucked my way through college, through most of my teenage years, and not one woman has ever lingered inside my head past my final nut in them. I've never gotten jealous.

Until now.

It's why I find myself in this mess.

A literal mess.

Exhausted whimpers finally reach my ears over the rapid thudding of my heart, blood rushing in my ears as breath heaves its way in and out of my chest. Crimson paints me up to my elbows, red splattered across my chest, blood dripping from my brow, the taste of it heavy on my tongue. But I've got what I came here for.

"You touched her," I spit at him, thinking of earlier, watching him, through the small circular window that looks into the music hall, sit down beside her and lay his hands atop hers. His body sprawled out beneath me, eyes glazed, brow and upper lip wet with sweat, "You just couldn't keep your fucking hands to yourself, could you?"

"Wh- who?" the man mumbles, his teeth chattering with shock.

"Ostara Stone," I hiss, lifting his severed hand and tossing it up in my palm to feel its weight.

"But I- I'm- I'm just her teacher!" the idiot yells, groaning, and clutching his arm to his chest, blood shooting out in small little spurts and lashing his chin.

"You teach piano, you don't need to be pressed up beside her and sliding your filthy fucking hands all over her!" I roar, spittle flying from my mouth where I'm crouched down over him, my shadow smothering the entirety of his rapidly expiring body. His eyes start to roll as I finish sawing off his left hand, "Now you won't be able to touch her ever again," I tell him slowly, calming my breathing with the affirmation.

Gathering myself up from my crouched position on the ground, back twinging as I straighten my six-foot-four frame. I swipe the back of my bloodied wrist across my forehead, pushing back fallen strands of my straight, brown hair, and stare down at the man bleeding out.

Fury bubbles beneath the surface of my skin as I head towards Ostara's room, amputated hands clutched tightly to my chest.

I need to show her.

She needs to know exactly what happens

when someone touches something that belongs to me without my permission.

Legs eating up the distance from the music hall to the dorms, I'm blinkered, blinded by rage. Taking the stone stairs three at a time, leaving little droplets of blood in my wake like a brutalised version of a gingerbread trail. I'm mad, enraged, feeling as though I could spit fire and burn this entire castle to the ground.

I don't worry about the butchered body I'm leaving behind in the music room, the state of me, covered in blood and carrying severed limbs, as I move through halls that are currently empty, but might not be for long. All I can focus on is Ozzie. The way she's avoided me for weeks, left me to die in the woods without ever seeking me out before straight up ignoring me altogether. Like a spectre, a ghost haunting this old building like a true night-mare, *my* nightmare.

And then today, I finally catch sight of her like a summoning from a spirit board, and that filthy slimeball tutor had his perverted fingers all fucking over her.

My fist hammers against her door, rattling the solid mahogany, it's an echoing boom in the long corridor, the ceilings high and illuminated by flickering wall sconces. I grit my teeth, bashing my fist into the wooden barricade between us once more. My breathing is ragged, desperate sips of air filtering in through my barred teeth, nostrils flaring, and it's like I can smell her, even from out here, this dark, delicate scent teasing my senses. Everything about her dizzies me, images of her writhing on my dick flash through my mind and I imagine that night all over again.

If I could take a screwdriver to my temple and twist the memory out of my skull, I would, but as it stands, I'm feral over protecting that moment. Even after the fact when she told me it was *fine*.

I've hunted her since, skulking through the shadows, spending hour upon unhealthy hour watching her room, stalking her classes, for any sign of her. There's been nothing. It was as though she didn't exist in the world for the last however many weeks. Everyday felt longer, every painstaking second seemed to drag like a dull blade down the insides of my wrists. Teasing and useless and providing no satisfying outcome.

I step away from the door and do the only thing I can.

Ram my way through it.

Pain explodes in my shoulder as I finally break through, bursting into the dark room. A single bed dressed in purple sheets is pushed up into the corner behind the door, and there's a desk beneath the window overlooking the courtyard. I push open the door to my right that leads to a small bathroom that's empty too. Bright orange light floods the opposite side of the room, multiple glass tanks perched on a large, metal shelving unit that lines the entire left wall.

The hands thud to the floor as I let them go, ignoring the way they bounce on the stone flooring, and walk over to the shelves. The orange glow is from heat lamps, keeping the snakes inside the glass units warm. There are so many different ones, most of them hiding from view, curled beneath bark and hidden inside little caves made of rock.

Absently, I drop into a crouch, fingers finding the glass of the largest tank on the bottom shelf, the tail end of a yellow and black striped snake exposed in a nest of crunchy dark leaves.

"That's a Banded Krait," my little ghost informs me as she enters the room silently, her warm breath feathering down the side of my neck where she bends forward, a severed hand held tenderly between her fingers. "Are these Professor Dubois' hands?" she asks innocently, as though this is normal, finding a teacher and a pair of severed hands in her dorm room.

My eyes slide up to hers, her face cast in the warm glow of the heat lamps, her cheeks shadowed, hollowed out further by the uneven light in the room. She doesn't look at me as she leans over my shoulder, her attention on the snake even as she fondles her piano professor's hand.

"Where the fuck have you been?" I spit at her, anger this living, breathing thing inside of me, it's as though every muscle in my body is locked up at her complete lack of reaction.

"They have a highly potent venom, neurotoxi-"

"You've been avoiding me," I growl.

"I wasn't aware we were emotionally invested enough to feel the absence of each other," she replies simply, a note of confusion in her tone.

A laugh bubbles out of me, a huff of irritation escaping my nose, "Oh? You weren't?"

Her eyes are slow in their slide to mine, the blue colouring of them like gold speckled sapphires in the dark, mesmerising. She blinks, just once, and then she scans her gaze over my face like she's taking stock, filing the image away for later. It gets my dick hard, those big fucking eyes on mine, her attention, all on me, intoxicating, it takes my breath away like a punch to the gut.

"You didn't die then," she says plainly, as though it's nothing more than a mere observation, like she feels nothing when it comes to the question of my existence one way or another.

I lick over my front teeth, clenching my jaw until my molars squeak, "Stop avoiding my question, where have you been?"

She holds my gaze, it feels like long, long seconds go by at a snail's pace and then speed up like there was no wait for her clipped answer at all.

"You broke my door, left severed limbs on my flo-"

Without conscious thought, I move. Springing up from the floor, my fingers and thumb squeeze the sides of her neck, my palm a shackle around the front of her throat. Air whooshes out of her in an *oomph* as I rush her backwards and her spine connects with the mattress as I shove her down. Knees bracketing her, I straddle her waist, one of her arms trapped between her side and my knee, the other free between us, limp on her belly.

"You've been avoiding me." Her chest heaves beneath me, her eyes wide, but she doesn't even look mildly concerned. "Why?"

The tips of Ozzie's fingers graze my thigh, her eyes dropping to watch her hand moving to stroke across the inside of my leg. Even with jogging bottoms on this time, the material thick, her touch scorches and scalds my skin like we're bared to one another.

"I haven't," she replies quietly, her gaze still tracking the subtle movement of her fingers.

Her pulse is strong and steady beneath the tight grip of my fingers, heart an even beat beneath my other palm pressing flat to her sternum, nothing indicating a lie, other than her lack of eye contact.

"I've just been," she tucks her bottom lip between her teeth, razing her front teeth over the plump, pink flesh, "busy." She gives a little shrug as she says it, as much as my pinning her will allow her to move. "Why do you care anyway?" she asks gently, in that soft way she always does when she's with me, it's a genuine question, not a sarcastic spit of a phrase intended to dislodge me or get me to fuck off.

But it's not a casual question to me.

Why the fuck *do* I care?

But images flicker through the forefront of my mind like they're stuck on a never ending merry-go-round. My dick, her blood, the blissed out glazing of her big eyes, the feel of her lips sucking my tongue, her cunt squeezing around my cock.

And just like that it seems obvious.

"Because you've infected me."

"Infected you?" she questions, finally giving a reaction then, flicking her gaze up onto mine, a slight grimace tightening the slant of her mouth.

"*Mmm*," I hum, holding her gaze, rocking myself over her, my cock thick and hard against her belly. "You made me sick."

"Sick," she repeats like a statement as opposed to a question, blinking hard.

"Yes, Little Ghost, sick." I flex my fingers around her throat, shifting my other hand up her chest, catching the weight of her tit in my palm, my thumb grazing over the sharp point of her nipple pressing through the fabric of her sweatshirt. "Sick in the head, sick in the heart, sick in the soul."

I say it like a mantra, lowering my gaze to watch my thumb circle her nipple before dropping my head down to bite it. Ozzie hisses as I bite and then suck on her through the material, her dark, seductive scent filling my lungs, black cherries and something more, her free hand lifting to the nape of my neck, fingers curling into my hair.

Her back arches, pushing her chest up higher, like an invitation to feast, but I don't push my way beneath her clothes, I don't give into the insane impulses of my cock. Instead, I lick my tongue up the side of her neck, the tip of it skimming over top of my fingers and press my lips to her ear.

"You belong to me now," I inform her, nipping at her lobe, "so don't let anyone else touch you again, or those hands won't be the only ones in your collection," I whisper, lips skimming the sensitive skin beside her ear.

She gasps softly, her breath hot and humid against my cheek. I hover over her for another moment, revelling in the feel of her fingers against my skin, nails scratching gently over my scalp, then I push myself up and off of her. Leaving her sprawled out on her bed, with a heaving chest and a busted door. Stalking back down the hallways with the forbidden taste of her on my mouth.

Ostara

IV

Sick.

That one word bleeds uneasiness inside of me like lava spilling down the side of an erupting volcano. But Caelus didn't say it like it was a bad thing. He said it with a dagger-sharp possessiveness like he *liked* it, the feeling.

'Sick in the head, sick in the heart, sick in the soul.'

That's what I focus on now, as my skin itches, feeling too tight to really feel like my own, heart too heavy to beat its usual even, steady drumming like I've learnt to control so well, standing before my family's home.

Stone Hill Manor.

I think of all of the things Caelus has said to me since then. The secret meetings where sometimes we just talk, somewhere deep inside, what is known as, *Carnell Wood*. Other times he pins me in a darkened corner and ravishes me right there, where anyone passing by could see, and makes me see stars that definitely don't come from the sky.

I feel safe and protected and what I imagine *love* to feel like when I'm in the secure circle of his lean, muscular arms. He keeps me safe and makes sure I eat and get enough sleep. Caelus Carnell makes my heart flutter and my insides knot, and I'm supposed to hate him. He's supposed to hate me. But neither one of us does.

Guards let me through the gate without need for interaction, my white high tops soundless as I track my way up the thirty-plus stone steps to reach the front door which already hangs wide open. I didn't want to have to come back here ever, especially not like this, feeling the way I do right now.

Knowing what I've done and having no way of undoing it.

I suck a shaky breath in through my teeth, the cold air of the overly-air conditioned house making pain flare in my front two incisors as I cross the entrance hall, beelining straight towards the grand dining room.

Breakfast in this house, with these people, is never much more than a business meeting. Father assigns tasks, I nod in silent agreement, and then escape his vicinity as quickly as possible.

Colin Stone is not a nice man.

Zoe, the youngest at just sixteen, is the first of my sisters I see, short, white-blonde hair tucked behind her slightly pokey-out ears. Dark brown eyes lifting from beneath the heavy flutter of her lashes. She stares at me from her seated position at the far end of the table, on the opposite side to where I usually sit. When I take my seat, the room in silence with only her and I currently present, I see her left cheekbone is a bright burst of blue.

"Don't," she says immediately, rasping the single word across the surface of the shiny, black glass table top. "I deserved it."

I bite down on the inside of my cheek, holding her gaze, but if she says she did, I'm not going to argue. Zoe's the sister I'm the closest with, but none of us are closer than acquaintances, something else designed by our father. Besides, worse things have happened inside this house than a backhand to the face.

Our eldest sister, Amelia, is next through the door, our father close on her heels, and with no sign of our second eldest sister, Naomi, Colin begins to speak.

It's the usual stuff, the lists of small tasks he wants us to perform. His meaty hands plant on the table as he stands, pudgy fingers spread wide, he focuses his gaze on me, and it takes everything I have in me not to look away.

"A little birdy told me," he exhales, the small lump of his belly resting atop the table too now as he presses further forward, "you've recently become close with the Carnell *cunt*," he spits with disgust, and my entire skeleton twitches inwardly.

My heart clatters like tin lids crashing together, rattling my teeth, but I don't react, I don't even blink. I hold his gaze, the deep brown of his irises too much like my youngest sister's to hate them, but I can still hate how his gaze makes me feel, boring into me like a drill bit to the temple.

There's no one alive who has seen us together, realistically he shouldn't know that, but he's obviously found a way. I show nothing on my face, no outward reaction, but panic is like a piano wire around my heart, squeezing, squeezing, squeezing.

"Which makes your next job easier, Ostara," he says merrily, a little glint in his gaze, behind the lenses of his glasses, something stares back at me like joy, only this fleeting moment is filled with sinister and bloody intent. "You're to kill Caelus Carnell."

The rest of breakfast went by in a blur, the two tiny bites of bagel feel like rocks in my stomach, but Colin Stone's very real threats ignite sickness in my gut, the taste of acid sits heavily on the back of my tongue.

'You're sick, Ostara. Make sure you don't forget what we do to girls in this family that are sick like you.'

It doesn't matter that his order goes against the agreement between our families, because despite my grandfather and Cal's arguing like toddlers over some meaningless land deeds, they signed an agreement that neither bloodline is to cause harm to or kill the other.

It's why I don't think. Panic this very real, living, breathing thing inside of me, poisoning me from the inside out. My leaden feet carry me through the old stone halls, my white high tops splattering with red where it drips from my closed fist. I thought it would help, slicing my skin, letting it out, this overwhelming feeling tightening at my temples, squeezing my lungs.

It always usually helps.

The flats of my bloody palms collide with huge, wooden, double doors, fingers flexing and pushing them open with a rushing thud as the left one collides with the wood panelled wall behind it.

'You belong to me now.'

Caelus' hazel eyes narrow as his head snaps toward the interruption of his class. And there's a moment, suspended, where there's nobody else inside this studio as he stares at me.

Mirrors line the two adjoining walls where Cal stands in the furthest corner. Tall, muscular body angled towards me; his left hand curled around the long pine coloured barre bolted into the long mirrored wall. Upper half drenched in a thick sheen of sweat, his light skin exposed in the gaping neck and arm holes of the loose, black, stringer vest he wears, glistens under the harsh white lights. Black tights sculpted to his legs, silky black pointe shoes on his feet, extending the already long length of his legs into some-thing powerful and elegant. He's magnificent, every single inch of him.

That's one of the reasons he's so deadly.

His hazel eyes scorch me, burning me up from the inside out, and every instinct inside of me tells me to go to him. To tear my way across the wooden floors, ignore every student in this room, all of their gazes focussed in on the intruder interrupting their scheduled training session, and go to him.

But even as I will it, my brain sending urgent signals to my feet to get them to move. I'm frozen in place, every muscle, bone and inch of sinew locked in position. And the only thing I can get out when I look at him, like really, really look at him, with damp brown hair sticking to his forehead, his lips slightly parted as he stares at me, is his name.

"Caelus." It's shaky and low and uncertain and it's met with hushed murmurs and whispers at hearing me finally speak, break my own personal vow of silence whilst at this academy, but there's not enough time to process that either, because Cal's only concern right now, in the middle of his afternoon class, seems to be me.

"Class is over, everyone out," he booms the order, the sound of his thunderous voice bouncing around the huge hall.

Immediately, sweeping his way across the floor, students rushing past me to exit. It's an almost theatrical display, the way he moves, gliding over the wood, but there's concern in his eyes, warm honey-hazel freckled with dark, forest green, beautiful really, especially when his attention is solely fixed on me. I'm sick, coming here, to him, seeking... I don't even really know.

But I know we have something, even if I'm not fully certain what.

The doors shut with an echoing slam at my back making me flinch as Cal's hands find both sides of my face, "Ozzie," he breathes, his eyes searching mine, his hold on my face tilting my chin up. "What's wrong?"

His fingers flex against my cheekbones, my lips parting to speak, but nothing escapes me bar a heavy sigh, an exhale of relief. Caelus sweeps his warm thumbs up the length of my cheekbones, pushing the tips of his long fingers into my hair, holding onto my skull, like my head being cradled in his hands is where it belongs.

"You," is what I breathe out, a tiny sound, but one that feels heavy, like it holds all of the world's chaos and violence and death. "You-he- I'm supposed to-"

"You're crying," Caelus whispers, almost in awe, staring at my lower lashes as they clump with drops of despair. His palms are hot and clammy on my cheeks, thumbs smoothing over my skin, smearing the salty tears beneath my eyes. "Tell me what happened."

"I don't want to kill you," is my answer, all of my father's threats tumbling around inside my brain and making me physically ache.

He blinks, heavy black lashes shuttering over his warm eyes as he surveys me, and then his dark brown brows lift high on his head, "I'm your next kill," he says quietly, coming to the right conclusion with no help at all from me.

"I'm not doing it," I tell him, even as sickness washes around inside my belly, and bile climbs its way up my oesophagus like it's a creature made of sludge using hooked talons to ascend. "I don't care what happens to me." It's a breathless confession, one I don't have to think about, it's just true.

I think of the room, of the box, of the leather straps and the neck needles. The darkness and the light, the blasts of heat, of ice.

I'm stiff, my eyes wide as Caelus drags me into his chest, folding his arms over my back, hands cupping my head and shoulder like I mean something. My arms hang by my sides because I don't know how to do this, to *feel*, to hug, to cuddle. I've never been held before.

"Ozzie," he whispers into my ear, ruffling my hair with his breath, his sweat-slicked skin sticks to my clothed body, and his mouth is hot and wet when it presses to the side of my neck. "Put your arms around me, Little Ghost. Hold onto me while I hold onto you." Summoned, my arms slowly raise, my fingers curling into the loose fabric of his top, fisting in the damp cotton. "That's it," he hushes, soothing me enough to let my eyes fall closed. "Just hold onto me and I'll keep you safe."

Caelus

V

I'm getting increasingly irritated by having to hunt this -*my*- girl down. She is quite literally never where she says she is, that is, when she actually bothers using the phone I bought her. One her father doesn't know about and can't use to monitor and track her.

I can hardly concentrate as I storm through the halls, students and faculty alike flitting out of my way as my boots carve the way for me.

It's musty and dry in here with a nose

wrinkling undertone of something damp, everything is worn and wrinkled and well used, everything, except for her.

Ozzie has her back lightly resting against the full stacks, shelves stretching up all the way to the ceiling, filled with leather bound books, tomes and novels. Feet crossed at the ankles in the farthest corner of the library, my girl flips the page in the large book open in her hands, her blonde hair curtaining her face where her head dips forward, neck curved allowing her to read.

Her long fingers are barely visible beneath the pulled down cuffs of her oversized white sweatshirt, just the tips pinching the fragile paper as she turns another page.

Without warning, I creep up the aisle, and step right up into her. Crushing the book between our chests, her arms still folded over it, elbows digging into my abs. She peers up at me as I fist the shelf directly above her head, her eyes flicking to the tops of their sockets, head tilting back to glance up at my hand as my other cups the side of her neck.

She flinches, like she always does, any touch, any touch with affection seems to be almost confusing to her. Ostara Stone has been conditioned to believe that touch is only intended to cause pain or subdue a target, I'm going to keep proving to her that it's not.

In only weeks we've gone from a desperate hate fuck in the woods our families are at war over, to being tethered in ways I can't even attempt to put words to.

Breath rushes out of her as she melts into the hard juts of shelving at her back, my body overwhelming hers and pinning it in place, our fronts flush, the thick, hard length in my joggers digging into her belly.

"Ozzie," I tilt my head so my mouth is slanted over hers, not quite touching, but close enough that I could. "You're twenty minutes late," I hush, allowing my lips to gently pluck at hers with every word.

Her breath is warm against my skin, my hazel eyes on her bright blues, she looks at me now, with something like admiration, and it's like a baseball bat hits me in my sternum, "I didn't check the time."

"You didn't miss me enough today, Little Ghost?" I tease, the corner of my mouth curling up in a smirk before the sudden spark of alarm in her gaze compels me to explain. "I was only joking," I frown, stroking the rough pad of my thumb along the underside of her jaw. "I was worried, that's why I came looking for you."

Her eyes soften, lids shuttering over the sapphire blue, and she tilts her head, quickly pressing her lips to mine before she pulls back, the crown of her head gently connecting with the edge of the wooden shelf.

"Thank you," she whispers, squeezing her fingers tighter over the top of the book squashed between us. Swallowing, she lifts her gaze back to mine, glancing left and right before focusing back on me once more, "I have to go back to my father's tonight," she informs me. Sighing softly through her nose, she shakes her head gently, "I've been called in to report on my progress with you."

There's real fear in her gaze, a tremor that seems to vibrate through her skeleton and into mine, "What aren't you telling me?" I press my fingers into the back of her neck, kneading the tenseness in her nape.

"Cal," she shudders, dropping her gaze

once more to the book in her hands. "I'm not…" she trails off, exhaling deeply.

"You're not what?" I clench my jaw so hard my teeth squeak, but I'm just completely fucking gone for this girl, I think I have been for a while.

"Not yours," she whispers, her low voice cracking as she swallows, the movement of the jump in her throat running through the base of my thumb where it rests against her neck.

"Not mine?" Hairs lift all across my skin, the feeling of ants marching across my flesh.

"I'm still his, my father's property," she breathes, holding my gaze, enchanting, that's what she is.

"You're not *his!*" I spit, hissing the final word with disgust.

I think of the man that fathered her, and I hate him, not because I'm supposed to, but because of everything I know about him and his treatment of his family, he killed his own wife, for fuck's sake. "You are mine, Ostara, in every fucking way a person can be claimed. You. Are. *Mine.*"

Her hands spring up from the book, the thick binding still wedged between us, even as it slips a little. Her cool fingertips press to the exposed skin at the base of my throat, her index fingers dipping into the hollow.

"I'm promised to another, Caelus," she whispers, guilt thick in every confessional word, but she obviously doesn't understand the lengths I would go to keep her.

"I know all about that," I scoff dismissively, "and I think you'll find you've got a rejection on your hands."

Her lips part, opening, closing and then opening once more, her head shaking, "What do you mean?"

"It's taken care of, Ozzie, that's what it means." She stares at me, wide eyed and wanting, and my hard cock kicks against her belly, "And as for your father, if you marry me, he won't be able to own you either."

Silence is thick between us as my words sink in. The families' agreement was not to gravely injure or kill any member of either family, but there was never anything in that contract that said our two houses couldn't be joined.

"Your father is already breaking the treaty by putting a hit on me, but using his own daughter to commit the act? It seems as though he's trying to get rid of you too, Ozzie." Her eyes flicker between mine, her fingers curling into the round neck of my cotton t-shirt. "He knows if you break the agreement that my family will come for you, not him, *you*. They wouldn't stop hunting you until they killed you, an eye for an eye, and he knows that, Ostara." I cup her face with both hands, pushing my fingers into her hair, tilting her head back so our mouths are touching, my lips brushing hers with every overly pronounced word, "Marry me, Ozzie, and I'll keep you safe forever."

Breath shudders out of her, her bright eyes shining with tears, and then her mouth is on mine, her lips moulding to my own, her tongue slipping between my teeth. Our kiss is like fire and ice, life and death, it's wrong and right, and everything it shouldn't be. Then she's pecking my lips, plucking at them with her own.

"Yes, Cal," she whispers, her fingers finding my face, cradling me in her cool hands. "Yes, Caelus, I'll marry you."

And then my tongue is fucking into her

mouth, the book trapped between us is thudding to the ground, one of my hands pushes up under her skirt, fingers curling into the lace of her knickers, I tear them down.

"I've been obsessed with watching you for the last two years, Little Ghost," I tell her through biting kisses, my hands going beneath her thighs and rucking her up, so she sits at my waist. "Everything about you drew me in, from the moment you showed up here, I was gone for you, I just wouldn't let myself act on it."

Her teeth dig into my lower lip, biting and sucking on the swollen flesh. She nips at my tongue, our teeth clashing, her hands squeezing my cheeks as she crushes her mouth violently to mine. I shove down my joggers, my hard cock springing free and immediately finding the slick heat between her spread thighs. I'm inside of her in a single, hard thrust, my length throbbing as she squeezes around me, fighting the intrusion even as she groans with pleasure, my fingers flexing on her arse.

"And then, there you were," I breathe out, our foreheads touching, "in the woods, with another man," she smiles at that, and my heart skips a beat. "Killing him with a poisoned kiss. A bringer of death." Her breath is hot against my skin as I fuck her slow and hard, the contents on the shelves at her back thunking with every hard thrust.

"You're the only person in the world who sees me," Ozzie whispers, drawing back from me just enough that she can look me in the eye without blurred vision from being too close. "I never wanted to be seen," she reveals in a breathless confession, "not until you."

My hips piston, fucking her harder and harder until books are vibrating along the shelves and thudding at our feet. Our lips come together once more, our tongues tangled and teeth savage as we ravage each other's mouths. I work my way down the side of her neck, sucking and marking her pale skin as she curls her hands over my shoulders and buries her face in the crook of my neck.

Her small huffs of breath escape her nose, a low whine catching in her throat. Heat blooms in my belly, fire licking at the base of my spine, my balls tighten and her cunt clenches around my cock pulling me deep.

"That's it, come for me now, come for me, Little Ghost," I hush.

Taking her mouth with mine, I swallow her cry, feeling her clench around me tighter and tighter until I'm coming too. The tip of my cock tapping at her cervix, I hold deep, spilling myself inside of her. With a low groan, our mouths fused together, my cum filling her up, she slows our kiss. Bringing her hands back to my face, cupping my cheeks, she breaks away with a lick of her tongue laving across my bottom lip.

Resting her head back against the shelf, she smiles softly at me, squeezing her knees against my ribs, the heels of her high tops digging into my lower spine.

"You really want to marry me, Cal?" she asks softly, still holding that tiny smile that spears me like an arrow through my heart.

"I really want to marry you, Oz."

Ostara

VI

It's nine-pm when I head into my father's house. The halls are empty, my sisters are absent and as I make my way to my father's office as instructed by the door-man. We have a plan, Cal and I. I'm safe now, he's not going to let anything happen to me, he's not going to let me be locked away again.

Even still, sickness churns in my belly, intestines twisting, stomach heavy. An omen. Fearful apprehension is a physical thing. Sweat beads along my hairline, a single drop drib-bling down my temple, running down my cheek and dripping down my neck at the juncture where my earlobe attaches just above the corner of my jaw.

The house is silent and a low buzzing hums in my ears, louder and louder, as I get closer to Colin's office. The door is open wide, everything a deep, dark mahogany, the smell of expensive bourbon and leather polish is ripe in the air, and the man I fear above all others is sat behind his desk.

Back straight, shoulders squared, he smiles at me as I appear in the open frame, a slash of violence across his thin lips, curled up at the corners like a circus clown.

"Ostara," he *tsks*, still smiling, but like he's severely disappointed in me.

Caelus is three minutes from here in a car with his brother, nothing is going to happen to me. I will not be locked up again inside this house.

I chant the thought like a mantra, reassuring myself of my safety. The thin, plain, silver band hugging my left ring finger feels foreign and suffocating. Marriage. It feels like too much, even though, at the same time, it feels freeing.

Caelus Carnell would never lock me away.

That statement alone is truth.

"Your blood results came back, and I wanted to talk to you about them," he says then, the smile falling into some sort of frowning concern.

But it isn't real. If it is, it's certainly not aimed at me and my welfare, I'm nothing but a pawn, I know the risks of using poisons and toxins, my father only has the family doctor test me so often so that he can keep me around for my killing skills. If I died, he'd have one less weapon in his arsenal, but also one less problem. Suppose he's not really that bothered either way.

"You haven't killed the Carnell cunt yet," he states, as if, I, myself, am wholly unaware of my failed mission.

"It goes against the treaty," I swallow, watching his face remain impassive, that's always when he's the most dangerous, plotting, all seeing, all knowing. "The entire Carnell clan will come for me; I'll never be safe. How will I continue my role in the family if I can't ever be safe outside of these walls?" I'm quietly spoken, my words soft, and I don't believe I'm safe inside this house as much as I wouldn't be outside of it, but he doesn't know I'm not a Stone any longer.

Being a Carnell puts me in even more danger inside this house, but outside of it, I think I'll be safer than I have been in my entire life.

I know my father knows all of this, everything that I said. That's what has me even more worried. He didn't cut me off, he didn't interrupt, he let me speak as though it were the last words I'd ever be able to voice.

"Are you sure that's the reason you haven't gone through with it, Ostara?" he asks me coldly, "fear?" a single brow lifting high. "It has nothing to do with the fact that you've been fucking the Carnell cunt and are carrying his baby?"

There's suddenly a buzzing inside my brain, corpse flies descending to feast. Everything falls away around me, like the earth is one big sinkhole, swallowing me deeper and deeper. Gravel laps overhead, like a foamy sea wave of grave dirt, and I'm not sure I remember how to breathe. How to do anything but stare unseeingly ahead and tremble.

His *hmph* of dark laughter has me blinking, my blurry gaze finding him, bringing me back to the room, as my body sways and my fingers cling onto the back of the chair before me to keep me on my feet.

"This is really something, Ostara," he chuckles deeply, his belly jumping with the heavy sound. "You didn't know," he states it on a wheeze, the chuckle becoming real humorous laughter now. "I thought that was why you brought the boy with you, because he was protecting his heir."

Panic squeezes my lungs, choking me as the sickness in my belly rushes up the back of my throat, filling my mouth, and I'm bending over, throwing myself to the carpet. Just in time to scrabble my way to the waste paper bin in the corner of the room on my hands and knees and expel the contents of my stomach.

Colin cocks his head at me as I fall back onto my bum, heaving for breath, and propping my back against the wooden cabinet doors at the bottom of the bookshelves. I stare up at him, the way he is oh-so comfortable in his position above me, so he can look down at me, and I'll know my place.

His smile wide with teeth, he says, "But that's not what's going to be happening here tonight, daughter." He rises from his chair, unfolding his tall, pudgy body from the squeak of the leather chair before he crouches down in front of me, pinching the fabric of his slacks just above the knees and pulling them up. "First," he starts, licking his lips, "we'll wait to hear the explosion-"

"Explosion," I repeat, interrupting, hearing the word fall from my mouth but sounding absolutely nothing like myself.

"Don't interrupt, Ostara," he tuts casually, "As I was saying, we'll wait to hear the explosion and then we'll get you downstairs for Doctor Butler to take care of this little problem. Then, Ostara, *then* you will be marrying Matthew Griswold as arranged. You think your little boyfriend could deal with that so easily?" he laughs again and it's haunting, the way I feel the evilness inside of him drilling into my bones. "All that's done is change which Matthew Griswold you'll be marrying. *Senior,* which is probably perfect for you, a much older man, he has a firm hand, he'll knock you into shape in no time."

It takes seconds for this all to sink in, but it feels like water running off of my skin, nothing sinks in, nothing really penetrates, not until the house shakes, the entire foundation vibrating, and then I hear it. As my father grabs my upper arm, dragging me to my feet and yanking me out into the hall.

Deafening finality.

The boom.

Caelus

VII

Lungs wheezing with inhales of dense smoke, I hack a cough.

"Em," I choke, smoke tasting like coal on my tongue, extinguished fire in the back of my throat. "Emilius?"

"Cal," my eldest brother responds with a wheeze.

Prying my streaming eyes open, I can see nothing but heavy grey clouds filling the car. My restraint is still strapped across my chest, but I'm hanging, and I know we're upside down, the car flipped.

"Fucking hell," my brother groans, just before his hand lands on my shoulder, giving me a gentle squeeze. "You alright?" he coughs, his fingers tight, it helps me relax a little, confused and dazed, but it's like my brother's touch pulls my soul back into my body.

"Yeah," I huff out, my nose filled with soot. "You?"

"Well, I'm not having a fucking picnic," he chokes out with a laugh, the sound quickly strangled with a pained groan.

My fingers flex, uncurling and pressing against the roof. Turning my head, I look at my shattered window, the metal warped, bent, and see nothing but smoke billowing out of it and the dark night beyond. We're on a residential street, and despite there being only so many mansions set along it, it won't be long before the police arrive.

Ozzie is in one of them.

This isn't a coincidence.

My seatbelt is stuck, and it's pointless to keep hammering at the button to release it.

"Emilius," I start, choking and spluttering in my panic as more smoke billows from the crushed dashboard. "Can you get to your knife?"

"Yeah, yeah," he says, rustling fabric, I can't see him properly, but his hand drops from my shoulder and then it's back, a metallic snick loud in my muffled ear. "You want me to cut you down." he says without question, we've been in a position like this before.

Without responding, I press the flats of my hands to the ceiling, bracing myself for the seatbelt to disappear, readying to take my weight so I can crawl out of the window and get to my Little Ghost.

Whatever the fuck is happening in there, I can guarantee it's worse than being blown the fuck up.

"Ready."

The blade saws through the seatbelt awkwardly, the angle of Emilius' hand twisted and difficult, and it feels like I'll never get out, but then suddenly I'm free. And regardless of how prepared I am to tumble to the ground, or rather the roof, I seem to have no upper body strength and fall into a heap of myself.

"Jesus," I hiss, untangling my long limbs

and finding the jagged edge of the car window with my fingers.

I heave myself out, snaking my belly along the tarmac, coughing as I gasp, inhaling cold, clean air. My back heaves as I crawl around to my brother's side of the car, my eyes watering so much from the smoke I can hardly see. Then two small feet appear in the corner of my vision, and a young girl drops into a crouch at my side.

Short blonde hair, round brown eyes, terror twisting her features, her shoulders tremble, and I'm reminded instantly of my girl.

"I'm Ostara's sister," she tells me, "let me help."

I sort of collapse against the side of the overturned car, and she's reaching in through my brother's shattered window, murmuring things I cannot hear. My limbs vibrate, my muscles shaking, and my bones seem to throb with a confusing mass of pain and pins and needles, I can't quite decide if I'm injured or just in shock.

My vision blurs and my heart thuds slow, and I think of my girl inside that house, with a man that ordered her to kill me. But she wouldn't.

A smile lifts my lips, remembering her panic at the prospect, how she finally let me see her.

'You're the only person in the world who sees me.'

'I never wanted to be seen.'

'Not until you.'

I've seen her for too long, slowly getting closer, and then one day when I spoke to her, she finally responded, like she felt safe or trusted me. Perhaps she only replied to my incessant conversation because I was driving her up the wall.

I think of her breath against my neck, her lips on my mouth, her tongue tasting my skin, and her cunt squeezing my cock.

But her smiles, those tiny curls of her pout, these secret things that are just for me, it makes my heart hammer inside the cavity of my chest.

My wife.

"His leg," Ozzie's sister says, suddenly slapping at my cheeks. "You need to stay awake, get up, you need to get up, I need you to help me with your brother."

She's tiny, this tall, slinky, stick of a girl, flushed cheeks and wide eyes, she reminds me so much of her sister even with brown replacing Ostara's blue.

"Hey!" she says again, making me blink and suck in a sharp breath, my lungs burning with the first real, clean inhale. "Help me, you need to get up."

Together, we drag Emilius out of the car, his huge, broad, muscular body twenty-stone of dead weight. He groans and heaves for breath, but he says nothing as we keep trying to free him from the mangled vehicle.

"Come on, Em," I pant, "help us out a little, mate, *Jesus Christ.*"

My arms shake the entire time. Ozzie's sister's cheeks blown out, she huffs and puffs as we each pull on an arm, Emilius' fingers curled loosely around each of our forearms. Knees bent, we pull steadily, and finally, as sirens blare in the distance, we get him out.

Right trouser leg shredded, the exposed expanse of my brother's thigh is painted crimson, a deep gash running down the length of it, revealing a sharp white piece of bone sticking out just above his knee.

"Fuck, Em-" I start, but he cuts me off.

Snarling at me through gritted teeth, "Go get your girl," he orders, "go get her, and bring her home."

Chest heaving, I stare down at him, Ostara's sister helping him straighten into sitting. Pulling my phone out of my pocket, I unlock it, dial my youngest brother, and then toss the device to Ozzie's sister.

"Romulus will answer, tell him to come and get you both."

Ostara

VIII

All of my life I have been subjected to the darkest parts of the world.

I remember when I was only six years old, my father beheading a man on our dining room table. Zoe was two. She had red splatter across her chin and bib, and she smeared it all through her white-blonde hair with chubby fingers, giggling as she did. Our mother was still here then, and I remember hearing Amelia telling Naomi that night that the man was someone Mother was having an affair with.

When I was ten, I killed a girl.

She was a few years older than me, a friend of Naomi's. The girl would constantly pull my hair, yanking on it, making my scalp sore, my neck ache. So I put crushed peanuts in a chocolate milkshake, offered it up to her with a striped paper straw and watched her suck them up. She was highly allergic and went into anaphylaxis. I left her fitting on the ground behind the brambles at the rear of the garden. They found her the following day, stiff and very dead.

When my father asked me about it, I said nothing and stared at him, unblinking, unbothered. He smiled, patted me on the head and told me what a clever girl I was, rewarded me with a lollipop and sent me out to play with Zoe.

As I got older, he had me do more, always poisons, toxins, druggings. I never got my hands dirty, I never had to bludgeon anybody, never had to learn martial arts or self-defence, not like my sisters did. But I liked it, the killing, watching the different concoctions rush through a body, fizzing and frothing and popping. I went too far, killing his favourite chef, just because I wanted to.

Colin Stone told me that day, when I was fourteen years old that I was sick.

'You're a sick, sick girl, Ostara, you're not beyond my control, little girl, and it's about time I taught you that lesson.'

That was when I was locked up. I didn't see the sun again until I turned eighteen years old and I was sent to Blackgrave Academy. That night, wandering through the woods my family and the Carnells were at war over, I met Caelus.

And even though it was night, the moon a silver sliver in the sky, stars hiding behind black rain clouds, I saw the sun.

In him.

And now I'm here, naked, strapped to the same metal table I've been laid on too many times to count, leather straps locked over my throat, forehead, chest, waist, wrists. Feet spread, knees bent, ankles bound, I am completely and utterly defeated.

"This won't take long, Miss Stone," Doctor Butler coos mockingly from between my legs, sending a shiver down my spine.

Goosebumps prick my skin, my nipples peaked from the icy chill of the room. I can hardly keep my eyes open. The thought of Cal being killed, only feet from me, in an explosion set by my father makes me want to die too.

He's the only one to ever see me, to *love* me.

He promised he would love me for eternity, in this life and the next, they weren't the vows he was asked to recite when he took me, only hours ago, as his wife, so I know he meant them.

Caelus Carnell loved me.

And after this, when the last little piece of him is taken from this earth, I will kill myself to be with him. *Them.*

Tears track down my face as I feel Doctor Butler running his fingers down the length of my thigh, his gloved hand cold and overly friendly when he reaches my sex. My fingers curl into fists at my sides, my teeth gnashing before I bite into my lip, sucking the blood from the broken flesh and swallowing it down.

A sob hitches my chest, and I've spent years ensuring I never cry in front of this man, but it doesn't matter anymore.

My entire body trembles, despite being tied down, the straps can't hold back a bone deep quiver. Pain lances through my chest, my heart squeezing as I choke on my tears. I fought for so long to get my freedom, doing things I never wanted to do, following orders whilst trying desperately to hang onto my autonomy.

It's all gone now.

The fight leaves me quicker than it should, the pain inside my heart echoing in my head, a thumping in my temples as I strain the tendons in my neck with my cries. I thought I was strong, I thought after everything, I could navigate the world and find my place in it. But I can't do that now, not without Caelus.

Sucking in a sharp breath as something enters me, I go still. Frozen on the table, my eyes ping open, and I stare up into the bright white light overhead. The low humming buzz of the strip bulb is like a screech in my ears. There's pinching, in my tummy, and-

The door ricochets off the wall as it smashes open, my eyes darting to the left to try and see who, but through my blurred vision I

only see a dark shadow rushing across the space and tackling the doctor off of his stool.

Doctor Butler grunts, the thing that was inside of me falling away with his touch, and it's like I can breathe. As though my head is pushing up above the rough waves of the sea, and I'm breaking through the surface of the water, inhaling my first real breath since I went under.

There are grunts and groans and fists on flesh, the doctor screams, and then he gurgles into silence. The seconds after that are long, and I hold my newfound breath to wait.

Is this all inside my head?

"Ozzie!" My feet slip off of the stirrups, my legs freed. Buckles clang and straps fall away and I'm hauled up into strong, lean arms. "*Ozzie,*" Cal breathes into my hair, his arms tucking me up into his chest, my toes just brushing the floor.

"I thought you were dead," I sob, tears soaking into his t-shirt, my fingers clawing into his back. "I thought he killed you," tears stream down my face, my sobs choking. Pressing my mouth to the bare skin of his neck, I inhale him, the dark, masculine scent of him, woody and deep calming my trembles. "We need to leave, we need to get out of here."

Caelus places me on my feet, my entire body wracked with tremors. My teeth chatter, clanging together and I can't get them to stop. Then he slips his t-shirt over his head, exposing all of his tight, toned muscles, obscuring my view of him as he pulls the smoke scented fabric over my own head.

That's when I finally get a chance to look at him and gasp, "Cal," I breathe, reaching up my shaky fingers to the cut in his temple.

There's blood drying down the side of his face, black smears all over his face and arms. I swallow dryly, threading my other arm through the short sleeve of Cal's t-shirt as he drags it down to my thighs.

"What did he do to you?" my lips quiver and my chin wobbles, and everything feels like it's too heavy to move through, sludge filling my brain cavity.

"It doesn't matter, everyone's fine. Are you okay, Little Ghost?" he asks, frowning.

Smoothing his hands over my head, pushing back my hair, cradling my face in his big hands as my fingers move to his bare chest, my palm sliding over his heart so I can feel it beat for myself.

I nod, drawing in a shuddery breath, as I count the steady thuds.

"Words," he whispers. Commanding, "are you okay, Ozzie?"

"I'm pregnant," is what slips out instead, Cal's fingers stilling on my cheeks. Panic fills me once more as I feel his heartbeat kick up, hammering now, kicking against my palm like it's trying to break free. "I didn't know," I confess honestly, worry filling me "It's not that I tried to keep it from y-"

Caelus' kiss startles me, his grip on my face knocks my head back and his mouth covers mine with violence. Cal kisses me so hard my teeth ache, and I don't know whether he's trying to make love to my mouth or destroy me. He dominates the kiss in a way that I can only kiss him back when he allows it, my tongue sneaking into his mouth to lick over his own. His lips maul mine, sucking and biting, and then he draws back so suddenly, leaving us both gasping, he presses his forehead to mine.

"Is it terrible of me to say I'm so happy?"

he breathes over my lips, feeding me his words. "But, fuck, Ozzie, I'm so happy."

Fresh tears lick my cheeks, and he's smoothing them away with his thumbs, pressing the wetness into my hair.

"You are?" I ask.

My eyes flick between his own, vision blurred at our closeness but I can still see the beautiful colour of them, rich hazel freckled with deep emerald green. Mesmerising.

"I am," he laughs, this choked, happy sound that fills my chest with warmth. "I know it's not ideal, right now, but, *Ozzie*, Little Ghost, fuck, I'm the luckiest man in the world right now." He smiles down at me, nuzzling our foreheads and I feel myself smiling too. "You're beautiful, Ostara Carnell," he breathes, smiling wider and staring at my mouth, "but you're even more beautiful when you do that."

Pain explodes in the back of my head and I'm wrenched back, my feet slipping on the tiles as I'm yanked by my hair back into my father's chest.

"Get your hands off my fucking wife!" Cal

shouts, lunging forward, but pulling back so sharply, he almost slips.

"Nah, ah, ah," Colin Stone hums, tutting at my husband, and yanking my hair tighter, my skin pulling so taut on my face that my eyes water, but I kick my legs, claw his skin, and then cool metal digs into my temple, and I instantly stop struggling. "You break into *my* house, touch *my* daughter, and suddenly think I'll take orders from you?" I can't see my father but I can imagine his expression, an eyebrow raised, a cocky smirk on his thin lips, a pudgy cheek dimpled. "Seems you don't realise just how in over your head you are, *boy.*"

"She is not yours, not anymore, old man, let her go, and give her to me," my husband sounds terrifying as he makes the demand, cold and calm and powerful.

A shiver rips its way up my spine so violently it makes my breath catch.

"Didn't you hear me, you Carnell *cunt,* get the *fuck* out of my house!" my father bellows, jamming the gun harder into my skull, making me whimper, my toes barely grazing the floor where he yanks me up higher by my hair.

"Oh," Cal chuckles, tucking his hands casually into his pockets, "I heard you."

His rich eyes flick over Colin's shoulder before settling on mine, and then my knees are hitting the floor, the gun is going off, forcing a terrified scream to tear from my throat. Cal's hands are on my waist, his fingers digging into my ribs, hauling me towards him away from the open door my father was standing in at my back.

Cal drags me back towards the metal table I was lying on, both of us on the floor to witness my father drop to his knees, the gun clattering to the floor as his fingers just sort of give up gripping it.

Blood blooms in the centre of his forehead suddenly, it appears like a fast dribble at first, this deep, rich red trickling down the length of his nose. And then it starts to run in rivulets down his face, over his open eyes, parted lips. He gasps, this sharp, ugly, wheezing sound, and falls forward, face first, his arms not going out to attempt to save himself. His face smashes into the tiles at my feet, blood pooling in a puddle around him as I stare at the perfect, round hole in the crown of his skull.

Zoe stands in the open doorway, her chest heaving, eyes downcast on our dead father. There's a silver gun in her hand, one I've seen her use many times before, something she never leaves the house without.

"You can be free now," she says quietly, calmly, even as her entire body trembles, she speaks softly, like she always does. "*We* can be free now."

EPILOGUE

ONE YEAR LATER

Watching my wife hold our daughter makes my heart ache in ways I never knew it could. The sun is shining on them where they sit on a red picnic blanket in the overgrown grass of my family's home, both heads of white-blonde hair glistening in the sunlight.

We moved out of here a few months ago, buying our own house just four houses down, it has a big garden and a little fish pond, flowerbeds in the front. Ozzie likes to be outside, to breathe in fresh air, come rain or shine, she's out there, staring up at the sky, or shoving her hands into the earth, weeding and watering and planting new life. She says it's because she's free now, and only when she was set free could she enjoy it, the world.

"Never thought you'd be the first one married *and* a father, little brother," my older brother Novian laughs, tracing a finger around the rim of his whiskey glass.

"Mm, well, *I* never thought you'd still be voluntarily playing bodyguard to a girl almost twenty years younger than yourself," I shrug, his fist collides with my shoulder, a smirk on my mouth as I lift my glass and take a sip.

"Shut the fuck up, you know it's only because Emilius demands it," Novian grumbles, knocking back his two fingers of whiskey and banging the glass down to refill it.

"I'm not complaining. Besides, it makes Ostara feel better, knowing her little sister is safe from their family." Tension forms in my forehead, my brows creasing with it.

The girls' older sisters have taken over the Stone family and whether by some sort of twisted sense of duty or actual want for revenge, they're doing everything they can to take down the girl who killed their father.

Even if she happens to be their little sister.

"Em thinks she saved his leg," Novian mutters, swallowing hard as my eyes come to his.

Emilius has had problems walking since the explosion, since it broke his femur in three places and shattered his tibia.

"Perhaps she did," I reply, looking down into my glass.

"Perhaps he just wants a reason to keep her here," Novian whispers.

Head snapping up, I blink hard, staring at him, wondering what he means by that. But before I can ask, Zoe is striding through the back door, her bodyguard close at her back. The big fucker stops at the edge of the decking, watching her as she bounces her way past us without a greeting and makes her way down the wooden steps, jumping the last two and skipping through the grass towards her sister.

"Well, she is a good killer," I say absently, watching my wife smile.

Fuck, all this time and that's all it takes,

one smile from her, even if it's not for me, and my dick gets hard.

"Yeah," Novian scoffs, shaking his head before raking his fingers through the dark strands, but when I glance over at him, his eyes are still on Zoe. "Sure, *that's* what it is." His chair scrapes back, drawing the attention of the girls, "See you later," my brother grunts and then he's disappearing inside the house, slamming the door at his back.

I stare after him, my eyes boring into the tinted glass of the kitchen door. Nothing can be seen through it, but it's as though I can still feel him there, just on the other side of the door, staring out, at *her*.

"Cal," Ozzie whispers, soft arms sliding around my neck from behind, her breath fanning my cheek as she rests her chin on my shoulder. "I love you, husband," she tells me with a coy smile, pressing a kiss to the side of my throat and then laying her cheek on her arm to stare at me.

Leaning my head back into her shoulder, I turn my face towards hers, taking her lips with my own, I make sure to press my words into her skin, "And I love you, wife, forever and always."

When we kiss, it's hard to believe we're here.

Being born into hate for one another because it was in our blood. Because it was our duty. As easily as breathing we were to think of each other as the enemy. And now we're here, joined by marriage, by blood, our lives forever intertwined. I know my soul could never find another like hers for as many lives as I shall live. Because the two of us are wrong.

Wicked and broken and violent.

But together, together, we're something else, because her and I are the same.

She's sick.

Sick like me.

THE END

Afterword

Thank you so much for reading! I hope you enjoyed Cal and Ozzie's short story. If you're wondering what happens next for Zoe, keep your eyes peeled for her full length standalone story, *Sick Like Us* coming soon!

Also By
K.L. Taylor-Lane

SWALLOWS AND PSYCHOS

KYLA-ROSE SWALLOW

A Dark, Mafia, Why Choose Romance

PURGATORY

PENANCE

PERSECUTION

SWALLOWS AND SAVAGES

CHARLIE SWALLOW

A Dark, Mafia, MMF Romance

RUIN

ROT

TBC

THE BLACKWELL BROTHERS

HUNTER BLACKWELL

A Dark, Gothic, Horror, Stepsibling, MF Romance

HERON MILL

HERON MILL TENEBRIS

THORNE BLACKWELL

A Dark, Gothic, Mafia, MF Romance

ROOK POINT

WOLF BLACKWELL

A Dark, Gothic, MF Romance

CARDINAL HOUSE

ARCHER, ARROW, & RAINE BLACKWELL

A Dark, Gothic, Why Choose Romance

MAGPIE MANOR

STRYDER BLACKWELL

A Dark, Gothic, MF Romance

TBA

·

THE ASHES BOYS

A Dark, Bully, Gang, Why Choose Romance

TORMENT ME

BURY ME

IGNITE ME

·

RAVEN RIDGE HALLOW

BILLY BLACKWELL

A Dark, Gothic, Horror-Gore, Cult, MF Romance

HAUNT

LOVESICK

BRAM BLACKWELL

A Dark, Gothic, Horror-Gore, Cult, MF Romance

DEATHWISH

TOLLY BLACKWELL

A Dark, Gothic, Horror-Gore, Cult, MMF
Romance

HEARTLESS

GORE BLACKWELL

A Dark, Gothic, Horror-Gore, Cult, MF Romance

CRUCIFY

·

STANDALONES

NOXIOUS BOYS

A Dark, College, Bully, Why Choose Romance

SICK LIKE ME

A Dark, Gothic, MF Romance

SICK LIKE US

A Dark, Gothic, Age Gap, Why Choose Romance

SINISTER BOYS

A Dark Why Choose Romance

DELIRIUM

A Dark Gothic Romance

·

Where To Find
K.L. Taylor-Lane

WEBSITE - www.kltaylorlaneauthor.com

BOOKBUB - @KLTaylorLane

AMAZON - K. L. TAYLOR-LANE

INSTAGRAM - @kltaylorlane_author

TIKTOK - @kltaylorlane.author

PINTEREST - @KLTaylorLane

FACEBOOK - K. L. Taylor-Lane Author

GOODREADS - kltaylor-lane

FB READER GROUP - K's Southbrook Psychos –
Reader Group for K.L. Taylor-Lane

Content Listing

Mental Health, Manipulation, Graphic Sex, Graphic Violence, Self-Harm, Cutting, Virgin FMC, Poison, Murder, Mutilation, Graphic Gore, Blood Play, Slapping, Age-Gap (14 years), Student/Teacher, Enemies-to-Lovers, Suicidal Ideation, Snakes, Pregnancy, Amputation, Marriage, Mentions of Parental Abuse/Neglect.

This list is not exhaustive - although every effort has been made to include all potential triggers, there may still be other content in these pages that may be found triggering or upsetting to some